TRACTOR MAC
LEARNS TO FLY

Written and illustrated by

BILLY STEERS

FARRAR STRAUS GIROUX · NEW YORK

TRACTOR MAC AND SIBLEY THE HORSE

lived on Stony Meadow Farm. They shared the work and often shared their thoughts.

"Do you ever wish you were doing something different, Mac?" asked Sibley one afternoon. "Sometimes I think it would be fun to pull a circus wagon in a parade or maybe a trolley car full of people."

"I am happy being myself," answered the big red tractor. "Why would I want to be something I'm not?"

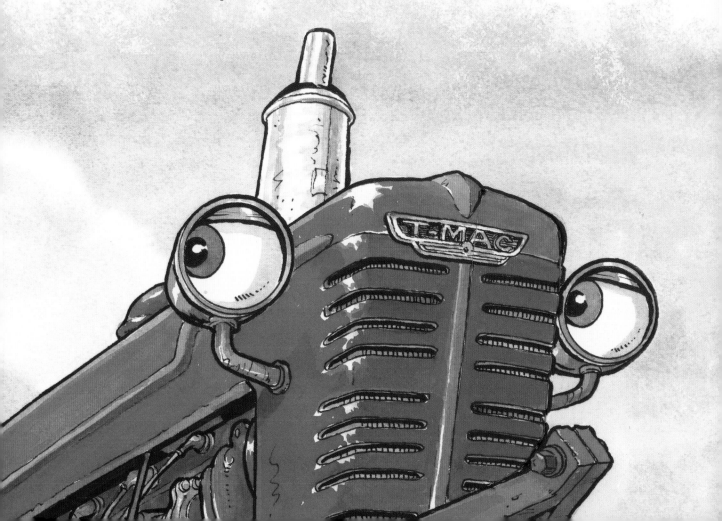

Just then, the two friends heard a sound that was quite different from Mac's normal chugging and popping. It roared overhead as it came near.

"Clear the runway!" a bright yellow airplane
shouted as it circled low over their heads.

Tractor Mac stared as the plane bounded
to a dusty stop in the hayfield. He had never
seen such a beautiful machine.

Smiling passengers climbed out while others stood in line to get on board.

Mac's heart fluttered with excitement. "That plane gives hayrides in the sky!"

Mac wheeled over to the plane.
"What's your name?" he asked.
"My name is Plane Jane,"
said the yellow plane.

"It must be wonderful to fly with the birds! Do you think I could do that?" asked Mac.

"No, you couldn't," she answered. "You don't have any wings, so how could you fly? Ta ta. Off I go into the wild blue."

For the rest of the day, all Mac could think about was flying. What a thrill it must be!

That night, Mac told his story of the bright yellow plane to the birds on the farm. Mac asked them a lot of questions about flying. They talked until late into the night.

Day after day, Mac looked at Plane Jane as she flew overhead with a new load of thrill seekers. Soaring, gliding, looping, rolling. As Mac watched, he longed more than ever to fly.

Then one day, quite by accident, Mac's big chance came. As he was chugging down the hill from the pumpkin patch, something snapped.

SNORT! *PING!*

His brakes stopped working. The heavy load pushed Mac faster and faster. He was rolling down the hill out of control!

He could not stop! *ZOOOOM!*
Suddenly, Mac was flying . . .

. . . for a little while. **SPLOOSH!**
Mac plunged into the pond.

Sibley came along and pulled him out of the water. "You were right, Mac," Sibley said. "You should be happy with who you are."

"You bet!" Mac agreed. "Leave the flying for the ducks, geese, and Plane Jane. From now on, my place is with my big black tires planted firmly on the ground."